TRON

BETRAYAL

Library of Congress Cataloging-in-Publication Data on file.
ISBN 978-1-4231-3463-3
First Edition
10 9 8 7 6 5 4 3 2
Printed in the United States of America
V381-8386-5-11007

Visit www.disneybooks.com
www.Disney.com/Tron

Certified Chain of Custody
35% Certified Forests,
65% Certified Fiber Sourcing
www.sfiprogram.org

TRON
B E T R A Y A L

AN ORIGINAL GRAPHIC NOVEL PREQUEL TO
TRON: LEGACY

Disney PRESS

NEW YORK

WRITER **JAI NITZ**

PLOT **STARLIGHT RUNNER ENTERTAINMENT**

ART **JEFF MATSUDA & ANDIE TONG**

COLOR **PETE PANTAZIS**

LETTERING **JOHN J. HILL**

COVER ART **JOCK**

Based on characters created by Steven Lisberger and Bonnie MacBird
Story by Edward Kitsis & Adam Horowitz and Brian Klugman & Lee Sternthal
Screenplay by Edward Kitsis & Adam Horowitz
Executive Producer Donald Kushner
Produced by Sean Bailey, Jeffrey Silver, Steven Lisberger
Directed by Joseph Kosinski

+

PROLOGUE   6

CHAPTER ONE   18

CHAPTER TWO   72

EPILOGUE   118

DEVELOPMENT ART   126

+

PROLOGUE

BY JAI NITZ & JEFF MATSUDA

I AM **DUMONT**, THE KEEPER OF **RECORDS**, THE KEEPER OF **INFORMATION**, THE ORDAINED **STORYTELLER** OF **FLYNN, THE CREATOR**. IT IS HIS WILL THAT I RECORD THIS INFORMATION FOR HIS **DISC**.

FLYNN'S STORY BEGINS IN THE WORLD OF THE **USERS**, A CITY OF ANGELS AND **LIGHTS**.

FLYNN'S FIRST ACT WAS TO MAKE **LIGHT** IN OUR WORLD OF DARKNESS. HE BUILT US, BIT BY BIT.

FLYNN WAS UNLIKE THE OTHER **USERS**. HE WAS, AND IS, A **CREATOR**. HE MADE ORDER FROM THE CHAOS OF ONES AND ZEROES.

HIS FINEST CREATION, THE **MASTER CONTROL PROGRAM**, REBELLED AND TRIED TO **DESTROY** HIM. THE MCP BROUGHT FLYNN TO **THE GRID**.

TRON AND RAM HELPED FLYNN ESCAPE OUT OF THE GAMES AND ONTO THE GRID. BUT FLYNN'S OWN CREATIONS, THE **TANK PROGRAMS**, WOULD HUNT THEM DOWN.

FLYNN CREATED THE TANKS TO SERVE AS **PROTECTORS** OF THE INTEGRITY OF THE GRID.

LITTLE DID HE KNOW THAT **HE** WOULD ONE DAY BE THE OBJECT OF THEIR WRATH.

FLYNN AND RAM WERE HIT, THEIR LIGHT CYCLES DESTROYED. TRON BELIEVED THEM TO BE **DEAD**.

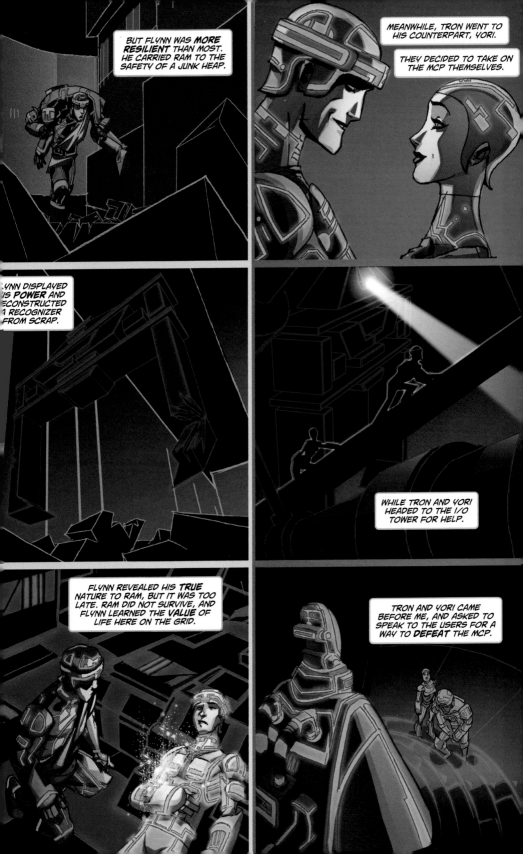

TRON, BRAVE AND BOLD, RECEIVED THE INFORMATION HE NEEDED.

TRON FOUGHT THROUGH SARK'S DEFENSES.

AND *REUNITED* WITH FLYNN ON A SOLAR SAILOR.

TOGETHER, FLYNN, TRON, AND YORI WOULD CHALLENGE SARK AND THE MCP.

BUT THE ODDS *DID NOT* FAVOR THEM.

MCP WAS A **POWERFUL** BEING. SARK WAS REBUILT AND REBORN WITH ENOUGH POWER TO OVERWHELM EVEN TRON.

THE MCP H. NOT PREPAR FOR FLYN IT HAD NO PREPARED I THE CREAT AND HIS GLO FLYNN CAS HIMSELF IN THE MCP

FLYNN CREATED A **HOLE** IN THE MCP'S DEFENSES, AND TRON **STRUCK.**

THE INFORMATION ON TRON'S DISC DESTROYED THE MCP, AND THE SYSTEM WAS FOREVER CHANGED.

THE OPPRESSIVE **RED** OF THE MCP GAVE WAY TO THE NEW **BLUE** BEAM OF FLYNN. AND FLYNN WAS **RESTORED** TO HIS USER FORM.

IN THE WORLD OF THE USERS, FLYNN REGAINED CONTROL OVER **THE SYSTEM**.

THE CREATOR, RETURNED TO HIS CITY OF USERS, WOULD GRACE US OFTEN. HIS GUIDANCE AND STEWARDSHIP USHERED IN A **NEW ERA**. AND SO ENDS THE GOSPEL ACCORDING TO DUMONT, THE GOSPEL OF **FLYNN'S DISC.**

the end.

CHAPTER ONE

BY JAI NITZ, STARLIGHT RUNNER ENTERTAINMENT,
ANDIE TONG, & PETE PANTAZIS

THE ROMAN EMPIRE STARTED AS A COLLECTION OF HUTS ON TOP OF SEVEN HILLS THAT OVERLOOKED A RIVER VALLEY.

THAT RIVER AND THE NATURAL SURROUNDINGS MADE ROME SAFE AND STRONG. IT HAD SOME HICCUPS ALONG THE WAY, BUT IT GREW AND GREW.

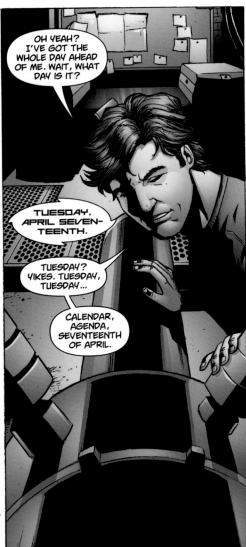

WOW, A BOY?

IT'S PRETTY HARD TO MISS, KEVIN.

YOU SHOULD HAVE SEEN IT. IT WAS MAGICAL.

IT JUST LOOKS SO GRAINY AND FUZZY.

I'M USED TO BETTER GRAPHICS. SOMEONE REALLY SHOULD INVENT A BETTER SONOGRAM CAMERA.

WELL, WHEN YOU'RE DONE WITH YOUR CURRENT OBSESSION, YOU CAN MAKE THAT YOUR NEXT PRIORITY.

FOR YOU, ANYTHING.

EVEN GRAINY AND FUZZY, IT WAS BEYOND ANYTHING I'VE EVER SEEN. IT'S A NEW LIFE. IT'S JUST...BEYOND ANYTHING I COULD EXPRESS.

I KNOW WHAT YOU MEAN.

NO ONE IS FROM THE WEST COAST. AT LEAST, IT SEEMS THAT WAY.

ALMOST EVERYONE HERE IS FROM SOMEWHERE ELSE.

TOMORROW'S SCHEDULE?

CONFLICTING APPOINTMENTS, SIR. YOU ARE DOUBLE-BOOKED AT NINE, TEN, ONE, TWO, AND FOUR O'CLOCK.

NOT ME. I WAS BORN AND RAISED HERE.

LOOKS LIKE I NEED TO BE IN TWO PLACES AT ONCE.

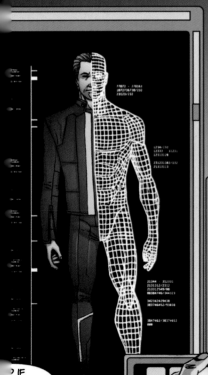

...D IF ...GNOSTIC ...S OUT, ...LY WILL ...E.

...CLU, ...N AND I ARE ...G TO CREATE ...E PERFECT ...SYSTEM.

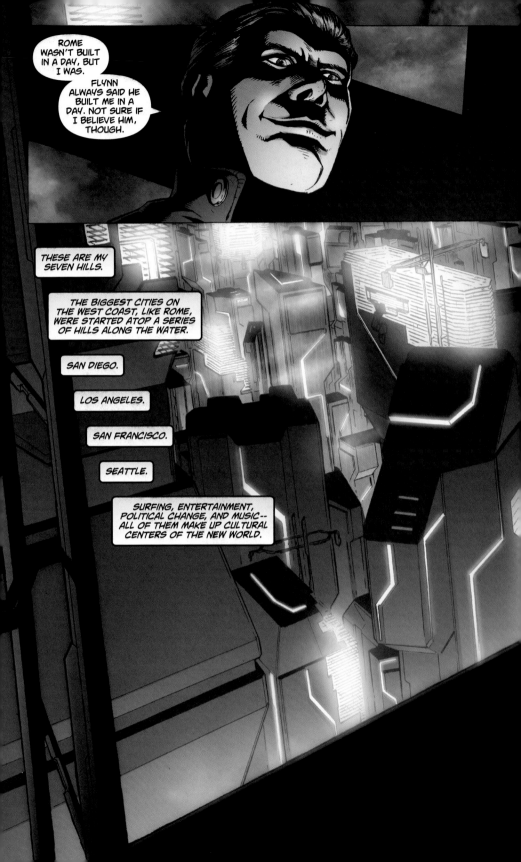

THE WEST COAST
MAKES MOVIES
AND VIDEO GAMES.

GOTCHA!

JORDAN, I FINALLY GOT IT TO WORK. NOW YOU CAN...

...CALL ME.

I WANTED TO HAVE FUN. I WANTED OTHER PEOPLE TO HAVE FUN. THAT WAS THE GRID'S ORIGIN. BUT NOW IT'S MORE THAN THAT.

CHAPTER TWO

BY JAI NITZ, STARLIGHT RUNNER ENTERTAINMENT,
ANDIE TONG, & PETE PANTAZIS

ZWAM

STEPPING AWAY FROM
ENCOM WAS A BIG CHANGE
FOR ME. I IMAGINED TRON
WAS GOING THROUGH THE
SAME KINDS OF CHANGES
THAT I WAS.

CLU! WE NEED TO TALK.

I THINK THIS POSITION WILL GIVE US THE OPTIMAL YIELD. YES. GO WITH THAT.

NOW!

TRON, WHAT AN UNEXPECTED PLEASURE TO HAVE YOU VISITING ME, WHAT WITH ALL THE TURMOIL ON THE STREETS AND THE VIGOROUSNESS OF THE GAMES.

THAT'S WHAT I'M HERE ABOUT. YOUR GUARDS WERE DEREZZING LOSING PROGRAMS AFTER THEIR MATCHES. DID YOU ORDER THEM TO?

YES. I DID. DO YOU WANT ME TO ALTER OUR NEW POLICY? I'D BE HAPPY TO DISCUSS IT WITH YOU.

THE GRID IS CHANGING, AND WE MUST BE THE SHEPARDS OF THAT CHANGE. WE'RE STARING INTO CHAOS, AND WE NEED

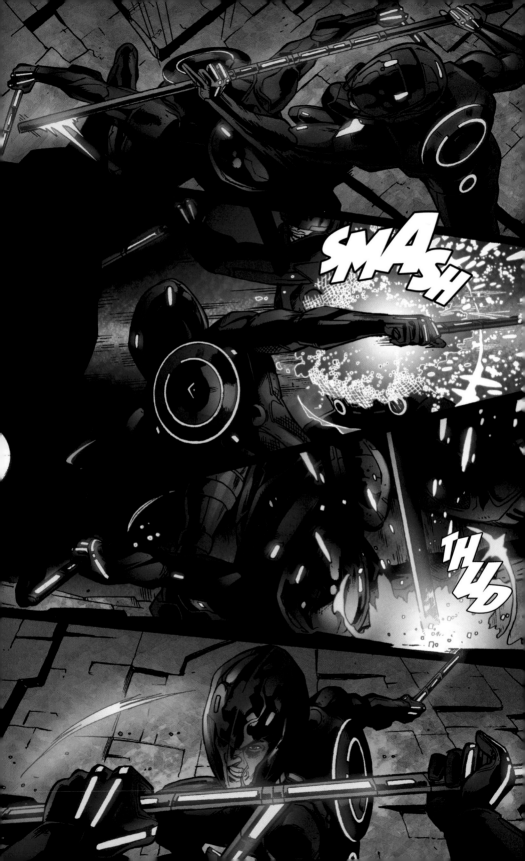

EPILOGUE

BY JAI NITZ, STARLIGHT RUNNER ENTERTAINMENT,
ANDIE TONG, & PETE PANTAZIS

1989.

THE BEGINNING.

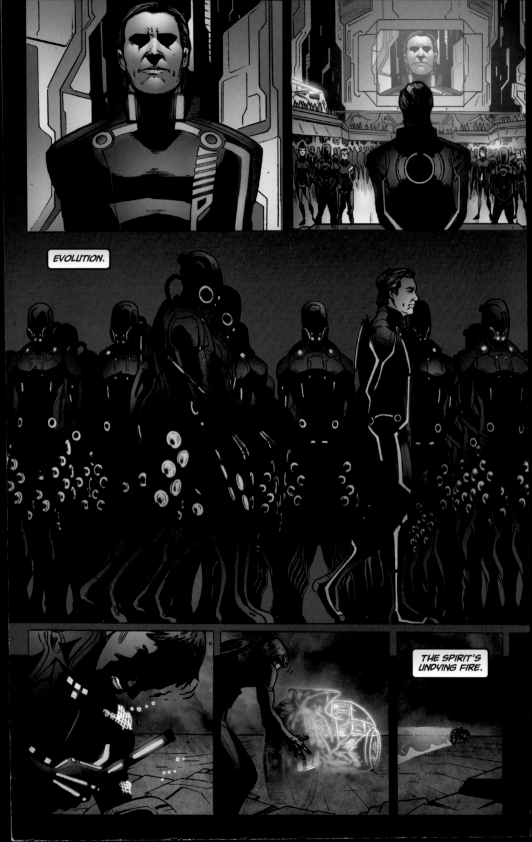

EVOLUTION.

THE SPIRIT'S UNDYING FIRE.

+

Turn the page for a quick download
of the process behind creating this
graphic novel. . . .

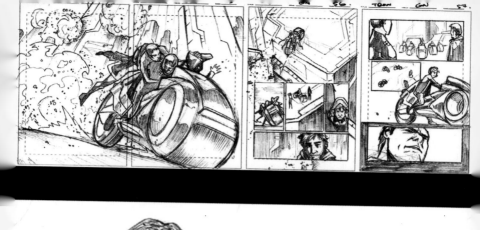

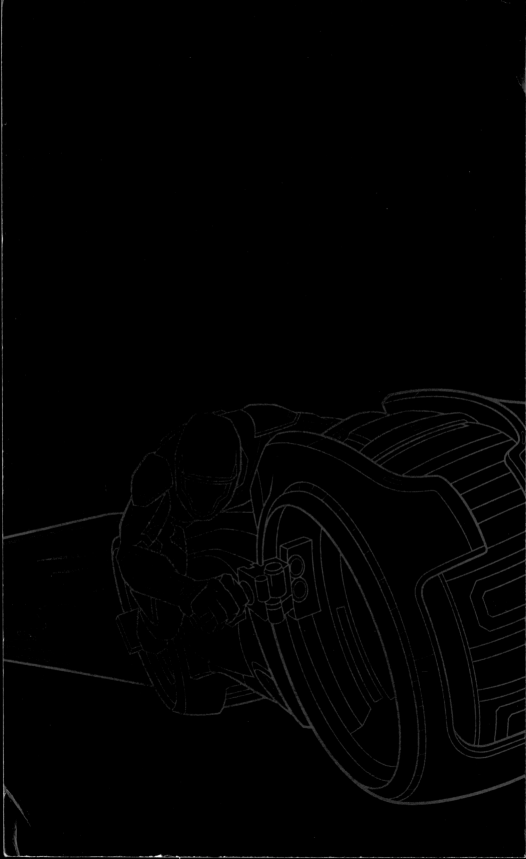